TO POOH,
WITH A LITTLE
GLUE AND LOTS
OF LOVE (AND A
SURPRISE INSIDE!)

ROO'S BEST GIFT

by Ronald Kidd
illustrated by Vaccaro Associates, Inc.

GROLIER
B O O K S

Based on the Pooh stories by A.A. Milne [copyright the Pooh Properties Trust].

Edited by Ruth Lerner Perle
Produced by Graymont Enterprises, Inc.
Design and Art Direction by Michele Italiano-Perla
Pencil Layouts by Ennis McNulty
Painted by Lou Paleno

ISBN 0-7172-8442-5

Printed in the United States of America.

Grolier Books is a Division of Grolier Enterprises, Inc.

Every year at holiday time, Kanga invited everyone in the Hundred-Acre Wood to an open-house party. She would serve delicious treats and everybody would exchange gifts. It was a happy time, full of fun, food, and friendship.

This year, a few days before the party, Roo had a dream. In the dream there were lots and lots of gifts for him, all wrapped in shiny paper and tied with brightly colored ribbons.

1

When Roo woke up from his dream, he hurried downstairs to find his mother.

"When do I get my gifts, Mama?" he asked Kanga.

Kanga smiled. "Soon, dear. You'll get your presents at our open-house party, along with everyone else."

Kanga took out her broom and mop and duster and started to prepare for the party.

As she did, there was a knock on the door.

Roo opened the door and Tigger came bouncing in.

"Hello there, Roo!" he said. "Let's bounce!"

"Yippee!" Roo shouted.

3

Roo and Tigger bounced around the house, laughing and playing.

4

When they were all bounced out, Roo said,
"Come on, Tigger, let's help Mama clean."
Roo helped Kanga sweep the floors by
climbing onto her broom and pointing
to the dirt.
Tigger helped her wash the
windows by following along
behind, rubbing his paw on the
glass to make sure it was clean.

5

After Kanga polished the table, Roo and Tigger used it for sliding. This was fine until Tigger slid off the edge and bumped his nose.

"Ouch!" cried Tigger. "I'd better go home now! Tiggers need to rest their noses after a hard day of sliding."

Tigger waved good-bye to Roo and Kanga. "See you at the party," he said.

6

Kanga sighed. Every year it was the same. Roo tried to help her with the party, but somehow he always got in the way. So this year, Kanga asked some friends to watch over Roo for a couple of days while she prepared.

On the first day, Roo visited Pooh.
When Kanga dropped Roo off, Pooh
was just taking a big jar of honey out
of his cupboard.

"Hello, Roo," Pooh called. "I'm
getting ready for your party. I've
decided to bring you my very best
jar of honey...just in case
someone happens to be in the
mood for a smackerel."

Pooh set the honey jar
down on the table and stared at it.
"Oh, bother," he said. "This
jar is too full. I'm afraid I might spill
some honey on the way to the party."
Pooh took a few licks of honey, but then the jar was
too empty. He added more honey, but then the jar was too
full again. So he took a few more licks of honey.

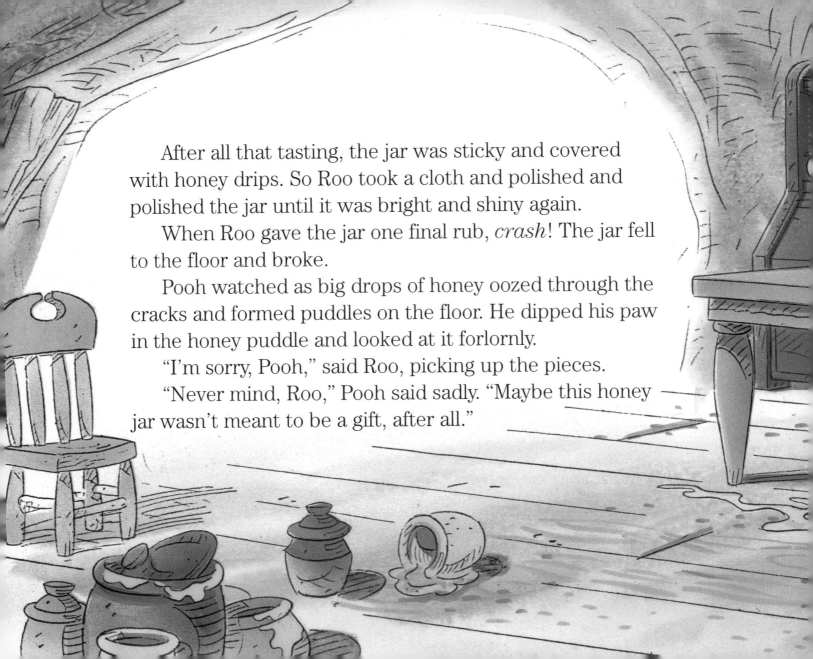

After all that tasting, the jar was sticky and covered with honey drips. So Roo took a cloth and polished and polished the jar until it was bright and shiny again.

When Roo gave the jar one final rub, *crash*! The jar fell to the floor and broke.

Pooh watched as big drops of honey oozed through the cracks and formed puddles on the floor. He dipped his paw in the honey puddle and looked at it forlornly.

"I'm sorry, Pooh," said Roo, picking up the pieces.

"Never mind, Roo," Pooh said sadly. "Maybe this honey jar wasn't meant to be a gift, after all."

11

After all the honey was cleaned up, Pooh put the
pieces of the broken jar behind his house. Then he came
back inside and played with Roo for the rest of the day.
But it just wasn't as much fun for Pooh because he kept
thinking about his broken jar.

The next morning, Kanga took Roo to spend the day with Piglet.

When they arrived at Piglet's house, there was a large box in the front yard. But Piglet was nowhere to be seen.

"That's funny," Kanga said. "Piglet knew we were coming."

"Hello," said a voice. It was coming from the box.

"Yippee!" Roo said. "A talking box!"

Grinning, he raced in circles around the box. When he looked at it again, the box had something else besides a voice. It had a head, and the head was Piglet's.

13

Piglet explained that he had heard about the accident with Pooh's honey jar. So he had decided to prepare for Roo's visit. He was filling a box with twigs, pine cones, and leaves for Roo to play with.

Roo cheered and hopped into the box. Kanga thanked Piglet and went home to continue getting ready for the party.

Later that morning, Piglet decided to make haycorn muffins. He and Roo could eat some of the muffins for lunch, and he could save the rest for the open house.

While Roo played, Piglet went into the kitchen. He got out his mixing bowl, flour, milk, and other ingredients.

Soon Piglet was ready to add the haycorns. He looked on the shelf where he kept them, but they weren't there. Then he remembered that he'd left them outside near the box.

15

Piglet ran outside and said, "Roo, have you seen my haycorns?"

But Roo didn't hear him. He was too excited about the string of ornaments he was making.

"See my decorations, Piglet." Roo said. "Mama can hang them over our door for the party!"

Piglet smiled. The ornaments looked very nice. There was something pleasing about their shape; something familiar. Then Piglet stopped smiling. Roo's lovely ornaments were Piglet's haycorns, held together with string.

When Piglet and Roo ate lunch that day, they didn't have haycorn muffins or anything else with haycorns in it. Roo thought the lunch was delicious anyway. Piglet was glad that the haycorn ornaments *would* make such a lovely open-house gift. But the rest of the day just wasn't as much fun for him.

The next day, Roo went to play with Eeyore. Roo found the old gray donkey standing guard by the thistle patch.

Eeyore said, "Don't come any closer, Roo."

"Why not?" asked Roo.

"Because thistles are my favorite thing," replied Eeyore. "I'm afraid something might happen to them, the way something happened to Pooh's honey jar and to Piglet's haycorns."

"Don't worry, " said Roo. "I don't even like thistles."

As they went off to play, Eeyore said, "I don't suppose you see anything different about me today, do you, Roo?"

"Yes, I do," Roo said. "It's that thing on your tail."

"Thanks for noticing," said Eeyore. "That's my holiday bow. I'll be wearing it to your party."

All morning, Roo played games with Eeyore. Roo's favorite game was sliding down Eeyore's back. One time when he was sliding, he reached out and grabbed Eeyore's tail.

Suddenly there was a ripping sound. Roo found himself lying on the ground, holding a donkey tail in his hands. The tail was torn from top to bottom.

21

"I'm sorry, Eeyore," Roo said. "Let me pin the tail back on for you."

Eeyore looked at the tail and shook his head sadly. "No thank you, Roo. I'm afraid it's of no use anymore."

22

Slowly, they walked back to Eeyore's house. On the way, Eeyore said, "You know, I just remembered. Thistles aren't my favorite thing. My favorite thing was my tail."

Eeyore and Roo played a few more games that afternoon. But Eeyore missed his tail and the rest of the day just wasn't as much fun for him.

Roo didn't go visiting the next day, because it was the day of the open house.

That morning, he helped Kanga arrange the gifts.

"What's in the gifts, Mama?" Roo asked. Kanga smiled, lifted Roo up to her lap, and sang a song.

What's in a gift beneath the bow
And paper tied with string?
It might be beads or cakes or seeds—
It could be anything.
But in each gift there's something else,
The most important part.
You put it there because you care;
What's in a gift? Your heart.

Roo thought about the words in the song. "I want to give some gifts, too," he said.

He told Kanga what he wanted to do, and they worked on the gifts for the rest of the morning.

Soon it was time for the party to begin.

The first guest to come bouncing in was Tigger, followed by a smiling Christopher Robin.

Owl was right behind, telling holiday stories to anyone who would listen. He even told a few when no one was listening.

Pooh, Piglet, and Eeyore arrived last, wishing everyone a happy holiday. But from the glum looks on their faces, it wasn't a happy holiday at all.

27

Everybody ate, drank, and sang holiday songs.

Then it was time for Kanga to hand out her gifts...a plate of holiday cookies for each guest.

But when everyone had a present, there were still three gifts left.

"Pardon me, Kanga," said Pooh, "whose gifts are these?"

Roo said, "These are from me. They're for three special friends who played with me while Mama was busy."

Roo handed the first package to Eeyore. Inside it was Eeyore's tail! It had been sewn up, good as new. There was a note that said: *To Eeyore, with a little thread and lots of love.*

Eeyore was so happy he didn't know what to say. So he just looked at Roo and then finally said, "Thank you!"

The second present was for Piglet. When he opened it, he found a basket of haycorn muffins! The note said: *To Piglet, with a little flour and lots of love.*

Piglet hugged Roo and said, "Now we have haycorn muffins after all. Thank you!"

29

The last present was for Pooh. Inside was his honey jar, with the cracks mended.

The note said: *To Pooh, with a little glue and lots of love (and a surprise inside).*

Pooh looked into the jar. It was filled with honey!

Pooh gave Roo a big hug. "Oh, thank you, Roo," he said. "You're a good friend."

As Pooh spoke, Roo felt a warm, happy feeling that went from the top of his head to the tips of his toes. That was when he knew that the best gift isn't wrapped in shiny paper or tied in brightly colored ribbon.

The best gift is the feeling you get when you've helped a friend, because giving is the best gift of all.

To Pooh,
with a little
glue and lots
of love (and a
surprise inside!)

31

POOH

PIGLET

EEYORE

TIGGER